For Matthew and Andrea
—E.F.

Annick Press Ltd.

We acknowledge the support of the Canada Council for the Arts, the Ontario Arts Council, and the Government of Canada through the Canada Book Fund (CBF) for our publishing activities.

ONTARIO ARTS COUNCIL
CONSEIL DES ARTS DE L'ONTARIO

Cataloging in Publication

Senior, Olive
    Birthday suit / by Olive Senior ; paintings by Eugenie Fernandes.

ISBN 978-1-55451-368-0 (pbk.).—ISBN 978-1-55451-369-7 (bound)

    I. Fernandes, Eugenie, 1943– II. Title.

PS8587.E552B57 2012   jC813'.54   C2011-907057-X

Distributed in Canada by:
Firefly Books Ltd.
66 Leek Crescent
Richmond Hill, ON
L4B 1H1

Published in the U.S.A. by Annick Press (U.S.) Ltd.
Distributed in the U.S.A. by:
Firefly Books (U.S.) Inc.
P.O. Box 1338
Ellicott Station
Buffalo, NY 14205

Printed in China.

Visit us at: www.annickpress.com
Visit Olive Senior at: www.olivesenior.com

Birthday Suit

Olive Senior
Paintings by Eugenie Fernandes

annick press
toronto + new york + vancouver

Johnny likes to run around
naked.

You would, too,
if you were almost four
and spent most of your time
outdoors,
in a nice warm place
where as soon as you awoke
you could run down
to give the ocean a poke
with your big toe and cry,
"Hello, sea. It's me!"

"**O**h, Johnny," says his mom,
"you can't go running around
with no clothes on.
You're too old
for that now.
You wear these
at least when you're splashing
and crashing and playing
in the sea.

Red swim trunks
are just the thing
for a big boy like you
to be seen in."

But as soon as his mom
turns her back,
Johnny strips down
to his birthday suit.

"Ha-ha, sea. It's me!"
he says.

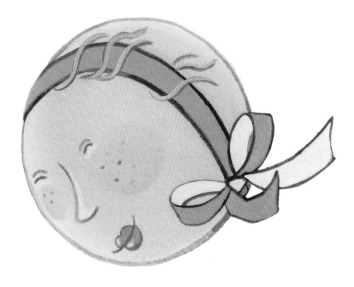

Johnny can undo
everything his mom uses
to lock him in:
buttons
bows
strings
zips
and
the thingamajig
that Johnny rips
with that lovely tearing sound.

Until . . .
one awful day
his mom comes home from
shopping,
and, holding up
overalls,
she points
at metal studding
all over them. Then she
holds two of these
evil metal monsters together
and says,
"This here is a genuine,
100 percent
shrink-proof
burglar-proof
hurricane-proof
child-proof
snap fastener
with a lifetime
guarantee
against
misuse!"

SNAP!

In a flash
she's
got the overalls
over Johnny and
with a
SNAP SNAP SNAP SNAP
the two ends
of each whatchamacallit
snap together
faster than a
turtle snapping,
and she's
FASTENED
him in!

"**WAAAAAA!**"
Johnny wails and cries
like a waterspout and yells
so loud
the tide rushes out
before its time
and the fish are turning
somersaults where they
ought not to
and the
whole world is spinning
around—
until . . .

Johnny's jellyfish squirming
slippery worming
jump-about jostling
writhing and tossing
find him free, with a
POP!

"Oh no," moans Johnny's mom
at the empty overalls.

"Oh no!"
roars the ocean
with a mighty heave.

His dad calls him:
"Come here, Son.
Let's have a talk
man to man.
One fact of life is,
big kids wear clothes
when they're out
in the great wide world.
Do you want to be
big like Dad?"

Johnny looks way, way, way
up at his dad,
and thinks that
almost touching
the ceiling
isn't such
a bad thing. For if he
grew that tall
he'd be able to
pick the ripest mangoes
at the top of
the tree
without ever
using
a stick.

So he nods
at the thought
and he puts on his overalls
and everyone
claps.

Peace at last.

"**Y**eah," says Dad, "you'll see.
The ocean will greet you
differently."
So said, so done.

From that day on,
Johnny has had such fun with
clothes . . .

taking them off
putting them on
zipping, unbuttoning
turning them inside out
tying and snapping
and running about.

Dad laughs at his clowning
as he puts him to bed
with socks on his fingers
and pants on his head.

When Johnny goes down
to the seaside now,
the ocean roars out,
"Who's the big lad, anyhow?"
"Ha-ha, sea. It's me," Johnny sings,
and the ocean waves back.

Johnny tumbles about
laughing,
little waves rush the beach,
the hidden crabs giggle
as he dances out of reach.

Now it's time for swimming.
Johnny's jumping in,
showing off his swimsuit
and happy with everything.